BLUE MEA...

...TTEN BY DAVE SMITH

...ED BY COLIN HARDY

Hubble & Hattie

KING OF THE STREETS!

The Hubble & Hattie imprint was launched in 2009, and is named in memory of two very special Westie sisters owned by Veloce's proprietors. Since the first book, many more have been added, all with the same objective: to be of real benefit to the species they cover, at the same time promoting compassion, understanding and respect between all animals (including human ones!)

Our new range of books for kids will champion the same values and standards that we've always held dear, but to the adults of the future. Children will love reading, or having read to them, these beautifully illustrated, carefully crafted publications, absorbing valuable life lessons whilst being highly entertained. We've more great books already in the pipeline so remember to check out our website for details.

OTHER GREAT BOOKS FROM OUR HUBBLE & HATTIE KIDS! IMPRINT

9781787116993

9781787115163

9781787113060

9781787113121

9781787114180

9781787114302

9781787111608

9781787112926

9781787115156

9781787113077

9781787113862

9781787117631

9781787117389

9781787117198

9781787117488

9781787117372

9781787117730

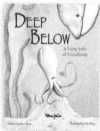
9781787117464

WWW.HUBBLEANDHATTIE.COM/HUBBLEANDHATTIEKIDS/

First published April 2022 by Veloce Publishing Limited, Veloce House, Parkway Farm Business Park, Middle Farm Way, Poundbury, Dorchester, Dorset, DT1 3AR, England. Tel: 01305 260068/ Fax: 01305 250479 email: info@hubbleandhattie.com/ web: www.hubbleandhattie.com ISBN: 978-1-787117-48-8 UPC: 6-36847-01748-4 © Dave Smith, Colin Hardy & Veloce Publishing Ltd 2022. All rights reserved. With the exception of quoting brief passages for the purpose of review, no part of this publication may be recorded, reproduced or transmitted by any means, including photocopying, without the written permission of Veloce Publishing Ltd. Throughout this book logos, model names and designations, etc, have been used for the purposes of identification, illustration and decoration. Such names are the property of the trademark holder as this is not an official publication. Readers with ideas for books about animals, or animal-related topics, are invited to write to the publisher of Veloce Publishing at the above address. British Library Cataloguing in Publication Data: a catalogue record for this book is available from the British Library. Typesetting, design and page make-up all by Veloce Publishing Ltd on Apple Mac. Printed and bound by TJ Books Limited, Padstow, Cornwall

DEDICATION

FOR NANCY, LUCY, SAM AND ADAM,
AND THE DRAG RACING FAMILY WORLDWIDE

MEANIE WAS A MUSCLE CAR WHO THOUGHT HE RULED THE STREETS.
FROM EVERY SET OF TRAFFIC LIGHTS, HE SURE WAS TOUGH TO BEAT.
HIS PAINT WAS ALWAYS SHINY, HIS EXHAUST WAS LOUD AND FRIGHTENING,
AND NOBODY COULD BEAT HIM, 'COS HE WAS AS FAST AS LIGHTNING!

He beat the local hatchbacks, he beat the Subarus,
all the Skylines and the Audis, he could beat them, too.
He could beat Ferraris, and even Lamborghinis,
and nobody could beat him because he was King Blue Meanie!

One Friday he was sleeping at home in his garage,
when up the driveway came the local cop car they called Sarge.
Sarge looked very angry, he was ready to explode.
He had photographs of Meanie driving too fast on the road!

"I know that you've been speeding, we caught you in our trap.
If I catch you racing on my streets, I'll haul you off for scrap!
The street is not the place to race, that isn't big or clever.
So go and find a race track or I'll lock you up forever!"

Sarge's words shocked Meanie, and he felt a proper fool.
Racing is a lot of fun, but prison isn't cool.
He'd been very lucky so far, he'd never crashed or failed.
But he couldn't be King of The Streets in hospital or jail!

He went out for a gentle drive, he was feeling very sad.
Beating other cars was the most fun he'd ever had!
He'd have to give up racing, and that really wasn't fair.
But suddenly he smelled racing fuel and tyre smoke in the air ...

He followed the scent to a drag strip, and this is what he saw,
a line of other cool, fast cars were driving through the door.
He joined the queue of other cars, and went in through the gates,
and everywhere he heard the roar of turbos and V8s!

Meanie looked around the pits, and couldn't believe his eyes ...
lots of racing cars and bikes of every shape and size!
Some had superchargers, and big slick tyres for grip.
They'd all come from miles around to race safely at the strip.

He saw them charging up the strip and thought, "That looks like fun.
But I'm the King of The Streets; I'll show 'em how it's done."
He barged into the line and cried, "I shouldn't have to queue ...
I'm the King of The Streets, and twice as fast as you!"

The car next to him in the line was very old and worn.
Her paint was dull and dirty; her seats were scuffed and torn.
She had no trim or carpet, there were patches in her floor.
And she had rusty bubbles in the corners of her doors.

"Hi," she said, "I'm Tina Green, I'm very pleased to meet you!"
"Hi," he sneered, "I'm Meanie, I'm the guy who's gonna beat you!"
They pulled round to the start line, and Meanie had to grin.
He was King of The Streets — he couldn't fail to win!

Both the cars pulled into stage, the Christmas tree went green,
and Meanie saw the empty space where Tina Green had been!
She had launched hard off the start line and now was way ahead ...
he knew he couldn't catch her — she'd left him there for dead!

He was so embarrassed that he couldn't show his face.
"I'm supposed to be the King!" he wailed. "I shouldn't lose a race!"
He went to Tina's pit and shouted, "This just isn't fair!
I looked really stupid when you left me standing there!"

"I've been racing many years," she said "I've learned to read the tree,
and with a little bit of practice you'll be just as good as me!
Don't worry that you didn't win, it's only your first go,
and if you like, I'll gladly teach you all you need to know."

"I don't need your help," he snarled, "I'll do it on my own!"
He turned his back, went to his pit, and sat there all alone.
He knew those other race cars would be very hard to beat.
But there's another way to win, thought Meanie.
I could simply cheat!

That night, when it was dark and quiet, and all the race cars slept.
Meanie tip-tyred silently as around their pits he crept.
He stole a lot of wheel nuts, and let air out of their tyres.
He hid all of their tools and switched around their sparkplug wires.

Next morning the announcer called, "Come on, folks, time to race!"
And Meanie laughed and laughed at the confusion round the place.
They had flat tyres and oil leaks that ran across the pits.
Some wouldn't start, some wouldn't move, and some just fell to bits!

Meanie looked so smug as he cruised slowly to the start.
He told the marshals, "All the other cars just fell apart!
They must be scared to race me, 'cos they know I'm number one.
But if there's no-one here to race, I suppose I must have won!"

He snatched the winner's trophy, and cruised off down the track.
But there was someone waiting in his pit when he got back.
King Henry owned the drag strip, and organised the races.
And he just stood there holding back a crowd of angry faces.

He said, "Something quite alarming has happened here today.
But I've been doing this job for years, and I suspect foul play.
Some cars have been messed with, and some things have been taken.
And all those things are in your boot, unless I'm very much mistaken!"

"You think you are the fastest, and you call yourself 'the King.'
But if you can't win fair and square, that doesn't mean a thing.
You don't get to be the champ by racing on the streets.
Cheaters don't make champions, and champions don't cheat!"

"Now clean up all the mess you've made, and I think it would be wise,
If you return the things you took, and then apologise.
Racers like to trust each other; we're all friends here at the track.
So if you can't play nicely, get out — and don't come back!"

MEANIE WAS EMBARRASSED, AND HIS HEADLAMPS BURNED WITH SHAME.
HE PROMISED THEM THAT HE WOULD NOT PLAY TRICKS LIKE THAT AGAIN.
HE GAVE BACK ALL THE THINGS HE TOOK, AND HELPED TO PUT THINGS RIGHT,
AND CLEANED UP ALL THE OIL AND MESS UNTIL QUITE LATE AT NIGHT.

MEANIE SLUNK BACK TO HIS PIT AND PARKED THERE, FEELING SAD.
HE THOUGHT THE OTHER RACING CARS WOULD STILL BE RATHER MAD.
SO MEANIE PACKED UP ALL HIS STUFF AND WAS JUST ABOUT TO GO,
WHEN TINA GREEN AND ALL HER FRIENDS CAME BY TO SAY 'HELLO!'

Tina said, "Let's start afresh, and if you want to stay,
You can race with us tomorrow, and we can race all day!"
Meanie was delighted, he said, "You're really very kind,
I'd love it if you'd teach me how to race ...
... that is, if you don't mind?"

They talked of tyres and burnouts, and how to get more traction;
they talked of springs and shocks, and things to speed up his reaction.
They talked of fuels, and oils and tools, and how he could go faster,
and when he should let off the gas and thus avoid disaster!

He asked them lots of questions, and they were all so nice,
and very, very happy to offer help and good advice.
For the first time in his life he listened and he learned:
these guys were really super-cool, as far as Meanie was concerned.

He woke up Sunday morning; it was sunny, warm and dry.
He spent the whole day racing under a beautiful blue sky.
The racers all encouraged him, and each time he went quicker,
and in the evening they gave him a racetrack bumper sticker!

They said he should be proud of what he had achieved,
and he'd had so much fun with them, he didn't want to leave!
All week long, Blue Meanie couldn't wait for the weekend,
to get back to the race track, and join his newfound friends!

All that summer, Meanie raced, and weekends just flew by.
He didn't often win a race, but he would always try.
As summer turned to autumn and the days grew cool and damp,
the racers counted up the points to see who'd be the champ.

At the last race meeting, there were trophies of all sizes.
Meanie whistled, cheered and yelled as winners got their prizes.
He cried "Congratulations!" to each and every one,
and thanked them all for all their help, and everything they'd done.

When all the winners had been crowned, one trophy still remained,
and Meanie looked quite puzzled until Tina Green explained.
"Because you've tried so hard, Meanie, and done so well this summer,
we all thought that you deserved the prize for Best Newcomer!"

Meanie stood there staring, he could not believe his ears!
As his friends all cheered for him, his headlamps filled with tears.
He'd never felt so happy, with his trophy on his wing,
and a cheeky kiss from Tina Green made him feel just like a ... KING!

Now, whenever Meanie's out, just cruising round the place,
and some car pulls up next to him and says, "Come on, King, let's race!"
Meanie calmly tells them, "Let's take it to the strip,
and if you beat me there then you can frame your timing slip!"

Glossary

BURNOUT
BEFORE THE START LINE, THERE'S AN AREA WHERE THE DRIVER CAN 'BURN OUT,' SPINNING THE TYRES TO CLEAN THEM AND HEAT THEM UP TO MAKE THEM STICKY TO GIVE BETTER GRIP

CHRISTMAS TREE
THESE ARE THE STARTING LIGHTS AT THE DRAG STRIP. WHEN BOTH CARS ARE AT THE STARTING LINE, OR 'STAGED,' THE STARTER WILL PRESS A BUTTON THAT GIVES THE 'GET READY' (THREE YELLOW) AND 'GO' (GREEN) LIGHTS

DRAG STRIP
A DRAG STRIP IS A STRAIGHT, FLAT STRIP OF ASPHALT OR CONCRETE; USUALLY A QUARTER OF A MILE (400 METRES) LONG, WHERE TWO CARS RACE, SIDE-BY-SIDE

GAS (GASOLINE OR PETROL)
SOME RACE CARS USE SPECIAL RACING PETROL, WHILE SOME USE ETHANOL, METHANOL OR EVEN NITROMETHANE, WHICH IS HIGHLY EXPLOSIVE! 'LETTING OFF THE GAS' MEANS EASING UP ON THE ACCELERATOR PEDAL IF THE CAR BEGINS TO 'GET LOOSE' (LOSING TRACTION, WEAVING OR DRIFTING LEFT OR RIGHT)

MUSCLE CAR
A MUSCLE CAR IS A MID-SIZE CAR, USUALLY AMERICAN, WITH A BIG, POWERFUL ENGINE

REACTION TIME
THE TIME BETWEEN THE GREEN LIGHT COMING ON AND THE CAR LEAVING THE START LINE. A REALLY GOOD DRIVER CAN HAVE A REACTION TIME OF JUST A FEW THOUSANDTHS OF A SECOND!

SPRINGS AND SHOCKS

THESE ARE PARTS OF A CAR'S SUSPENSION. ALL CARS HAVE SPRINGS TO HELP SOAK UP BUMPS AND KEEP THE TYRES IN CONTACT WITH THE ROAD. 'SHOCKS' IS SHORT FOR SHOCK ABSORBERS, OR DAMPERS, WHICH STOP THE CAR BOUNCING ON ITS SPRINGS. A CAR BUILT FOR STRAIGHT-LINE DRAG RACING WILL HAVE ITS SUSPENSION SET UP DIFFERENTLY TO NORMAL ROAD CARS, OR CARS BUILT FOR ANY OTHER MOTOR SPORT

SLICK TYRES

SLICK TYRES ARE SMOOTH WITH NO TREAD; PERFECT FOR VERY POWERFUL RACING CARS BUT USELESS IN THE RAIN!

SUPERCHARGERS AND TURBOCHARGERS

THESE ARE DEVICES THAT PUMP MORE AIR INTO THE ENGINE TO HELP IT PRODUCE MORE POWER

TIMING SLIP

AFTER EACH RUN, THE DRAG STRIP WILL GIVE ENTRANTS A TICKET THAT TELLS THEM THE TIME IT TOOK TO COVER THE QUARTER MILE, HOW FAST THEIR REACTION TIME WAS, AND WHAT SPEED THEY WERE DOING WHEN THEY CROSSED THE FINISH LINE

V8

MOST MUSCLE CARS HAVE A V8 ENGINE: AN ENGINE WITH EIGHT CYLINDERS THAT SOUNDS AWESOME!

Drag Strips in Britain

Santa Pod, Northamptonshire — www.santapod.com
Melbourne Raceway, Yorkshire — www.straightliners.events
Crail Raceway, Scotland — www.crailraceway.co.uk

Drag Strips in North America

There are drag strips all across America and Canada. Most information can be found from the two main sanctioning bodies: the National Hot Rod Association (www.nhra.com) and the International Hot Rod Association (www.ihra.com).

ABOUT THE AUTHOR AND ILLUSTRATOR

DAVE SMITH IS A MOTORING JOURNALIST FROM THE MIDLANDS, AND THE EDITOR OF STREET MACHINE MAGAZINE (UK). DAVE OWNS A FAMILIAR-LOOKING FORD MUSTANG ...

COLIN HARDY IS A FREELANCE CARTOONIST AND ILLUSTRATO, LIVING IN SOUTH WALES. HIS WORK APPEARS IN STREET MACHINE MAGAZINE, MOG MAGAZINE, AND GASSER MAGAZINE (USA), AMONGST OTHERS.

ALSO FROM HUBBLE & HATTIE KIDS!

Join Moggy the Morris Minor Traveller as he embarks on a fun-filled, interactive pirate adventure along the wild and wonderful Cornish coast.

Moggy is on the hunt for hidden treasure, and he will need your help to solve the clues left by cunning pirate Captain Redbeard. Journey from one landmark to the next, with clear illustrations to guide you, and a subtle palette that captures the colours of a timeless summer landscape.

Young children will enjoy exploring the 12 engaging picture puzzles again and again, on their own or shared with an adult, whilst Moggy's retro and friendly features, and an entertaining narrative, will see young readers bonding with this loveable character, who is full of praise for their help along the way!

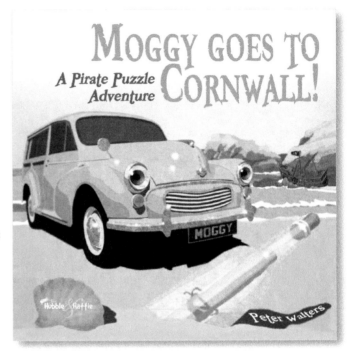

PAPERBACK ☠ 205x205MM ☠ 32 PAGES ☠ ORIGINAL COLOUR IMAGES THROUGHOUT
ISBN: 978-1-787117-73-0 ☠ £8.99* (*SUBJECT TO CHANGE)